Bilingual Books Collection

California Immigrant Alliance Project

Funded by
The California State Library

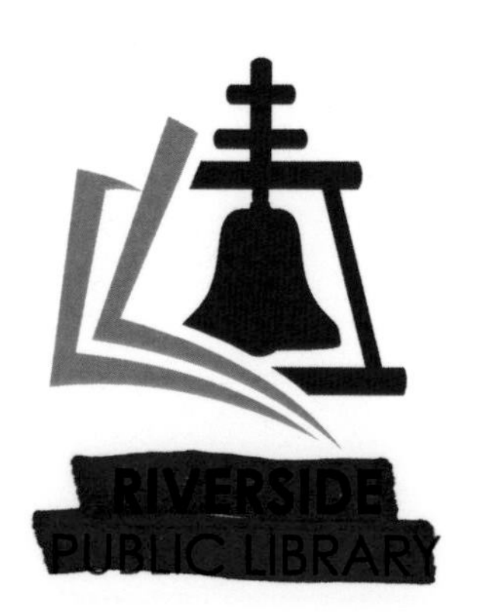

Celebraciones / Celebrations

Erin Day

traducido por / translated by

Fatima Rateb

PowerKiDS press

New York

Published in 2017 by The Rosen Publishing Group, Inc.
29 East 21st Street, New York, NY 10010

First Edition

Translator: Fatima Rateb
Editorial Director, Spanish: Nathalie Beullens-Maoui
Editor, English: Melissa Raé Shofner
Book Design: Michael Flynn
Illustrator: Continuum Content Solutions

Cataloging-in-Publication Data

Names: Day, Erin, 1986- author.
Title: Happy Mother's Day! = ¡Feliz día de la madre! / Erin Day.
Description: New York : PowerKids Press, [2017] | Series: Celebrations = Celebraciones | Includes index.
Identifiers: ISBN 9781499428445 (library bound book)
Subjects: LCSH: Mother's Day–Juvenile literature.
Classification: LCC HQ759.2 .D39 2017 | DDC 394.2628–dc23

Manufactured in the United States of America

CPSIA Compliance Information: Batch #BW17PK: For Further Information contact Rosen Publishing, New York, New York at 1-800-237-9932

Contenido

Contents

¡Hoy es el Día de las Madres!

Le hice una tarjeta a mi mamá.

Today is Mother's Day!
I made my mom a card.

A mi mamá le encanta estar al aire libre.
Le gusta caminar y también ir a la playa.

My mom loves the outdoors.
She likes to hike and go
to the beach.

Hoy mi mamá quiere ir al parque.

Recojo flores para ella.

Today, my mom wants to go to the park.

I pick flowers for her.

Vemos un carrito de helados.
El helado preferido de mi
mamá es el de fresa.

We see an ice cream cart.
My mom likes strawberry
ice cream best.

Mi papá extiende un
mantel. Nos sentamos
a disfrutar los helados.

My dad spreads out a big blanket.

We all sit down to enjoy our treats.

El cielo está lleno de nubes blancas y esponjosas. Veo una tortuga que pasa flotando. Mi mamá ve un tiburón.

The sky is filled with fluffy white clouds. I see a turtle float by. My mom sees a shark.

Caminamos alrededor del estanque de los patos.
Mi mamá me da la mano para que no me caiga.

We take a walk around
the duck pond.
My mom holds my hand
so I don't fall in.

Se me ocurre una idea de camino a casa. Le haré un regalo a mi mamá.

I have an idea on the way home. I will make my mom a gift.

Utilizo cuentas de colores brillantes para hacerle un collar. ¡A mi mamá le encanta!

I use bright beads to make a necklace. My mom loves it!

Ella me da un abrazo. ¡La mejor parte del Día de las Madres es pasarlo con mi mamá!

She gives me a big hug. The best part of Mother's Day is spending it with Mom!

Palabras que debes aprender
Words to Know

(las) flores
flowers

(el) collar
necklace

(el) estanque
pond

Índice / Index